Acting Edition

Beanstalk! The Play!

by Rosalyn Mihalko
and Donna Swift

No one shall make any changes in this title(s) for the purpose of production. No part of this book may be reproduced, stored in a retrieval system, scanned, uploaded, or transmitted in any form, by any means, now known or yet to be invented, including mechanical, electronic, digital, photocopying, recording, videotaping, or otherwise, without the prior written permission of the publisher. No one shall share this title(s), or any part of this title(s), through any social media or file hosting websites.

For all inquiries regarding motion picture, television, online/digital and other media rights, please contact Concord Theatricals Corp.

MUSIC AND THIRD-PARTY MATERIALS USE NOTE

Licensees are solely responsible for obtaining formal written permission from copyright owners to use copyrighted music and/or other copyrighted third-party materials (e.g., artworks, logos) in the performance of this play and are strongly cautioned to do so. If no such permission is obtained by the licensee, then the licensee must use only original music and materials that the licensee owns and controls. Licensees are solely responsible and liable for clearances of all third-party copyrighted materials, including without limitation music, and shall indemnify the copyright owners of the play(s) and their licensing agent, Concord Theatricals Corp., against any costs, expenses, losses and liabilities arising from the use of such copyrighted third-party materials by licensees. For music, please contact the appropriate music licensing authority in your territory for the rights to any incidental music.

IMPORTANT BILLING AND CREDIT REQUIREMENTS

If you have obtained performance rights to this title, please refer to your licensing agreement for important billing and credit requirements.

BEANSTALK! THE MUSICAL!, from which ***BEANSTALK! THE PLAY!*** was adapted, was originally produced at Island Theater Workshop's Children's Theatre in Oak Bluffs, Massachusetts in July of 2005. The performance was directed by Elizabeth Hight, with musical direction by Linda Berg. The cast was as follows:

NARRATORS . . . . Carolyn Hight, Lonnie Phillips, Sarah Tollman, Molly Gorin, Max Santos

JACK 1 . . . . Sam Permar

JACK 2 . . . . Vivian Ewing

JACK 3 . . . . Katy Gwynn

JACK'S MOTHER . . . . Katie Mayhew

COW . . . . Claire Hilsinger

SKUNK MERCHANT . . . . Samuel Graber-Hahn

CHEESE MERCHANT . . . . Grant Santos

POTPOURRI MERCHANT . . . . Elisabeth Bellissimo

BEANSELLER . . . . Taylor McNeely

THE ONE THAT GOT AWAY . . . . Genevieve Hammond

THE GIANT . . . . Katie Clarke

GIANT'S WIFE . . . . Tessa Permar

HEN . . . . Rose Capobianco

HARP . . . . Tessa Whittaker

MAGIC MAKERS . . . . Sarah Shaw, Eliana Grossman

CHARACTERS

NARRATORS 1-5 – The tellers of the tale.

JACK – A kind-hearted boy who believes in fairytales.

JACK 2 – Jack in disguise.

JACK 3 – Jack in another disguise.

MOTHER – Jack's mother; a grumpy old woman who used to be rich and happy.

COW – Jack's best friend.

ALEX THE SKUNK MERCHANT – A skunk merchant named Alex.

CHRIS THE CHEESE MERCHANT – A cheese merchant named Chris.

SUE THE POTPOURRI MERCHANT – A potpourri merchant named Sue.

BEANSELLER – A mysterious bean merchant with a secret past.

THE ONE THAT GOT AWAY – A fugitive in the magical land above the clouds.

THE GIANT – A big man with a big appetite for little people.

GIANT'S WIFE – A big woman with a big heart.

HEN – An enchanted and exhausted hen that lays golden eggs.

HARP – A magical singing harp who acts like an opera star/diva.

NOTE: JACK, JACK 2 & JACK 3 can be performed by the same actor. NARRATORS 1-5 can be performed by as many or as few actors as needed.

SETTING

The ordinary land below the clouds and the magical land above them.

TIME

The enchanted time of fairytales.

AUTHORS' NOTES

BEANSTALK! THE PLAY! is meant to be performed without blackouts. The scene breakdowns are for organizational purposes only. In the original production members of the cast used their bodies to form the various sets and furniture pieces. Most of the props, except for the signs and the storybook, can be actual or mimed.

Scene 1

(Setting: A Miserable Little Shack)

(At rise: **MOTHER, COW** *and* **JACK** *enter.* **JACK** *begins reading a storybook.* **NARRATORS 1-5** *enter.)*

NARRATOR 1. Once upon a time…

NARRATOR 2. There was a poor widow…

NARRATOR 3. Who lived in a miserable little shack…

NARRATOR 4. With a meager cow…

NARRATOR 5. And her only son –

MOTHER. JACK!

JACK. Oh, hello Mother. How are you this fine morning?

MOTHER. Thirsty. Have you gotten any milk from the cow yet?

JACK. Nope. Not yet.

MOTHER. All we have to eat around here is the milk from our cow, Jack. If you don't milk the cow, we don't eat.

JACK. Oh, Mother. You don't eat milk; you drink it. I read that in a book.

*(***JACK*** continues to read his book.)*

MOTHER. *(to* **COW***)* Ugh! What am I going to do with that boy? He sits around all day with his head in the clouds and his nose in a book.

COW. Moo.

MOTHER. His father was the same way and now all that's left of him is that stupid book of fairytales.

COW. Moo.

MOTHER. Well…I guess if you want something done you have to do it yourself. All right Cow, give me some milk.

COW. Mo.

MOTHER. What do you mean "No"?

COW. *(crying)* Moo-hoo-hoo.

MOTHER. You're out of milk?!?

(**COW** *takes out an empty glass milk bottle and turns it over to show it's truly empty.*)

COW. *(continues crying)* Moo-hoo-hoo-hoo!

MOTHER. Well, I guess we'll just have to sell you at the market then.

COW. Moooo?!?

MOTHER. Well, I can't sell the boy. JACK!

JACK. Yes, Mother.

MOTHER. You must go to the market and sell the cow.

JACK. But the cow's my best friend.

MOTHER. Too bad. We need the money to eat.

JACK. Oh, Mother. You don't eat money; you spend it. I read that in a book.

MOTHER. We're not going to eat the money, Jack! We're going to use the money to buy food!

JACK. If we need money, Mother, I can go and get some for us.

MOTHER. How are you going to get us money?

JACK. I'll go on a great, big adventure, just like one of the characters in my storybook. I'll find us a huge treasure and we'll never be poor or hungry again.

MOTHER. Nonsense. No good can come out of having an adventure.

JACK. What about the little girl on page twenty-seven? She had an adventure and she lived happily ever after.

MOTHER. That was a story, Jack.

JACK. This is a story too, Mother. This is our story. And today is the day that our dreams come true!

MOTHER. Fairy Tales aren't real, but our hunger is! *Now go to the market and sell the cow! And get a good price!*

(**MOTHER** *exits.*)

COW. Moo-hoo-hoo!

JACK. Don't worry, Cow. Everything's going to be fine, you'll see. Today really is our magical fairytale day!

COW. Moo.

(end of scene)

Scene 2

(Setting: The Market)

(At rise: **JACK** *is walking with* **COW**. **NARRATORS 1, 2 & 3** *enter.* **NARRATOR 3** *enters with sign saying "To Market" with an arrow pointing offstage.)*

NARRATOR 1. And so Jack went off to the market to sell the cow.

NARRATOR 2. It was a long and difficult journey.

*(***NARRATOR 3*** turns sign around so it says "Market!"* **NARRATORS** *1-3 exit. The* **MERCHANTS** *enter.)*

JACK. Well, here we are at the market. Wow! It's just like the picture on page thirty-four, only smellier.

ALEX THE SKUNK MERCHANT. Skunks for sale! The perfect pet for personal protection!

CHRIS THE CHEESE MERCHANT. Get your Limburger cheese here! Hold your nose and take a bite!

SUE THE POTPOURRI MERCHANT. Potpourri! Make the bees your new best friends!

JACK. Wow! Isn't this great, Cow?

COW. *(holding her nose)* Moo?

JACK. Well, I guess we better get to work. *(calling out)* Cow for sale! Meager, milk-less cow for sale! Will trade for food!

ALEX THE SKUNK MERCHANT. I'm sorry. Are you trying to sell that cow? At this market?

CHRIS THE CHEESE MERCHANT. Oh, that's just ridiculous. No one's going to buy that cow.

SUE THE POTPOURRI MERCHANT. Yeah, she's completely worthless.

(The **MERCHANTS** *laugh.)*

JACK. This cow isn't worthless. She's worth-full! She's one worth-full, wonderful cow!

ALEX THE SKUNK MERCHANT. Can she protect your home from burglars with her pungent spray?

CHRIS THE CHEESE MERCHANT. Or add a delightfully hideous aroma to your cheese plate?

SUE THE POTPOURRI MERCHANT. Or make your underwear smell like wildflowers?

JACK. No. I don't think so.

ALEX THE SKUNK MERCHANT. See? She doesn't do anything useful.

CHRIS THE CHEESE MERCHANT. You'll never be able to sell that cow.

SUE THE POTPOURRI MERCHANT. You'll be lucky to trade her for a sack of beans.

JACK. A sack of beans!!! Really?! That would be great!

ALEX THE SKUNK MERCHANT. Great?

CHRIS THE CHEESE MERCHANT. Really?

SUE THE POTPOURRI MERCHANT. Why would that be great?

JACK. You can eat beans! I read that in a book. Now where on earth am I going to find someone with a sack of beans?

*(***BEANSELLER*** enters with two great big buckets of beans.)*

BEANSELLER. Beans for sale! Extra ordinary and extraordinary beans for sale!

JACK. Well, that sounds promising.

BEANSELLER. Hello, Jack.

JACK. Hey, how do you know my name?

BEANSELLER. Oh, I know a lot about you, Jack.

JACK. Really? That's weird.

BEANSELLER. For one thing, I know you're looking to trade that cow of yours for a sack of beans.

JACK. Wow! You're just like that fairy-godmother lady on page seventy-three. Except you're a man. And you sell beans.

BEANSELLER. They're not all ordinary beans, Jack. Some of them are *magic beans*.

JACK. Wow! Magic beans! That's the kind of thing you'd find in a fairytale! *(gasp!)* Do you want to trade your magic beans for my cow?

BEANSELLER. I thought you'd never ask.

(BEANSELLER gives beans to JACK.)

Now remember Jack, these are magic beans…you must be very careful where you plant them…there's no telling what might happen.

JACK. Hey…that's just what the troll says on page eighty-seven.

BEANSELLER. There's more to life than words and pictures, Jack. Remember: life's an adventure that's meant to be lived.

JACK. That's just what the mysterious beanseller says on page ninety-four! Huh…that's weird. *(pause)* Well, I guess I better get going. Good-bye.

COW. Moo-hoo-hoo.

JACK. Don't worry, Cow. I'll come back and get you just as soon as I've had my great, big adventure! Today is our magical fairytale day!

(JACK walks away.)

BEANSELLER. I'm going to miss that boy.

COW. Moo.

(COW and BEANSELLER exit. NARRATOR 3, 4 & 5 enter. NARRATOR 3 has a sign that says "To Jack's House" with an arrow pointing offstage.)

NARRATOR 4. And so Jack took the five magic beans back home to his mother.

NARRATOR 5. It was another long and difficult –

JACK. Mother, I'm home!

NARRATOR 5. …journey.

(NARRATOR 3 sighs, turns sign around so it says "JACK'S HOUSE!" NARRATORS 3-5 exit.)

(end of scene)

Scene 3

(Setting: The Miserable Little Shack)

(At rise: **JACK** *is on stage.* **MOTHER** *enters.)*

MOTHER. Hello there, my darling boy. Did you get lots of money for the cow?

JACK. I did better than that. I got magic beans!

*(***JACK** *gives the magic beans to* **MOTHER.***)*

MOTHER. You traded our cow for these stupid beans?

JACK. Those *magic beans.*

MOTHER. You empty-headed boy! What have you done? Only a fool would exchange a cow for a bunch of worthless beans.

JACK. Wonderful beans! Glorious beans! Marvelous beans!

MOTHER. Enough with the beans!

*(***NARRATORS** 1-5 *enter.)*

NARRATOR 1. At the height of her exasperation, Jack's mother threw the magic beans out the window.

JACK. Mother! What are you doing?! Those are magic beans! There's no telling what might happen!

MOTHER. For the last time, there's no such thing as magic beans. Now go to your room!

NARRATOR 2. And so Jack was sent to his room without supper.

JACK. There's nothing to eat anyway.

*(***JACK** *and* **MOTHER** *exit.)*

NARRATOR 3. That night the most amazing thing happened.

NARRATOR 4. The magic beans began to grow…and grow… and grow.

NARRATOR 5. The stalks twined and twisted until they formed a gigantic ladder reaching far into the clouds.

(Beanstalk grows and grows and grows. **JACK** *enters with storybook.* **NARRATORS** 1-5 *exit.)*

JACK. Gosh I'm hungry. *(to stomach)* Don't worry stomach we'll find something to eat. Today is our magical fairytale day! (**JACK** *sees beanstalk.*) Wow! Would you look at that! A beanstalk! I've never seen anything like this before! Not even in a book!

(**BEANSELLER** *enters in flashback mode.*)

BEANSELLER. There's more to life than words and pictures, Jack. Remember: life's an adventure that's meant to be lived. Page ninety-four…

(**BEANSELLER** *fades away and exits.*)

JACK. He's right. This is my chance to have a great, big adventure of my very own. *(gasp!)* Today really is my magical fairytale day!

(**JACK** *puts down the book of fairytales and climbs up the beanstalk.* **NARRATORS** 1-5 *enter. One of the* **NARRATORS** *picks up the book of fairytales.*)

NARRATOR 1. And so Jack climbed up the tall and terrifying beanstalk.

NARRATOR 2. Higher and higher he went into the sky.

NARRATOR 3. It was like climbing a ladder to the stars.

(**JACK** *stops climbing the beanstalk.*)

NARRATOR 4. His mind raced.

NARRATOR 5. Where was he going?

NARRATOR 4. What would he see?

NARRATOR 5. When would he ever reach the top?

(**JACK** *clears his throat.*)

NARRATOR 4 & 5. Finally he reached the top.

(**NARRATORS** 1-5 *exit.*)

(end of scene)

Scene 4

(Setting: The Magical Land Above the Clouds)

(At rise: **JACK** *looks around in wonder.)*

JACK. Wow! A magical land above the clouds! This is exactly like nothing I've ever seen before.

*(***THE ONE THAT GOT AWAY*** *runs in screaming.)*

THE ONE THAT GOT AWAY. What are you doing up here?! Are you crazy? There's a man-eating giant on the loose! Run for your life! He's after us all!

*(***THE ONE THAT GOT AWAY*** *runs away.)*

JACK. A man-eating giant! How exciting! I better hide. Look, a castle! That'll be a great place to hide.

*(***JACK*** *enters the castle.)*

Wow, this castle is really huge! I wonder who lives here?

*(***GIANT'S WIFE*** *enters.)*

GIANT'S WIFE. A child! Can it be? My dreams have come true! Finally I have a child of my very own. *(to* **JACK***)* I will call you Mortimer and you will call me Mother.

JACK. But I already have a mother.

GIANT'S WIFE. You do? What are you doing here then?

JACK. I'm hiding from the giant.

GIANT'S WIFE. I'm sorry, but you can't hide here. It's much too dangerous. Now shoo. Get out of here. Shoo. Shoo.

JACK. I'm sorry, ma'am, but I can't shoo. I'm much too weak with hunger.

GIANT'S WIFE. Oh, you are so cute! Okay, I'll get you something to eat, but we'll have to be very careful. If my husband finds you here he'll eat you.

JACK. Your husband eats children?

GIANT'S WIFE. He's the giant.

JACK. Oh.

GIANT'S WIFE. He seemed so nice when we first started dating. He was so tall, and dark and handsome. And he said that he wanted children…I didn't know that he wanted them to eat.

JACK. Speaking of eating, I'm still very hungry.

GIANT'S WIFE. Well, I guess I could give you a quick bowl of milk.

JACK. Milk! Hurray! That's my favorite!

(**JACK** *sips the milk very slowly and very loudly.*)

GIANT'S WIFE. Go on now. Hurry up and be done with it.

JACK. If I drink too quickly I'll get hiccups.

GIANT'S WIFE. If you drink too slowly you'll get eaten.

JACK. Oh.

(**THE GIANT** *enters.*)

THE GIANT. Fee fi fo fum! I smell the blood of an Englishmun!

GIANT'S WIFE. My husband! *(to* **JACK***)* Quick! Hide!

(**JACK** *hides.* **THE GIANT** *enters.*)

THE GIANT. Wife! I smell a child!

GIANT'S WIFE. A child? Don't be silly. That's only a nice fresh steak of elephant that you smell. There, why don't you sit down and eat your dinner like a good giant.

(**THE GIANT** *eats his dinner in a very noisy manner.*)

THE GIANT. Wife! I'm finished with my dinner! Bring me my golden coins!

GIANT'S WIFE. Every night you count your stolen treasure until you fall asleep. We never talk anymore.

THE GIANT. Wife! Coins! Now!

(**GIANT'S WIFE** *gives golden coins to* **THE GIANT.***)*

GIANT'S WIFE. Fine. Here are your stupid coins. I'm going to bed.

(**GIANT'S WIFE** *exits.*)

THE GIANT. *(counting his coins)* One. Two. Three. *(***THE GIANT*** falls asleep.)* Snore!!!

*(***JACK*** comes out of hiding.)*

JACK. Gosh. That sure is a lot of gold. If we had just one bag of that gold we'd never be hungry again. I'm sure the giant won't miss just one small bag.

*(***JACK*** takes some of the gold coins. **NARRATORS 1, 2** *&* **3** enter.)*

NARRATOR 1. And so Jack took some of the giant's golden coins.

NARRATOR 2. He was very brave.

NARRATOR 3. Or very foolish.

NARRATORS 2 & 3. Or both.

*(***THE GIANT*** snorts and ***JACK*** and ***NARRATORS 1-3*** run off screaming and hide. **THE GIANT** wakes up.)*

THE GIANT. *(sleepily)* Giant. Bed. Now.

*(***THE GIANT*** yawns and exits.)*

(end of scene)

Scene 5

(Setting: The Miserable Little Shack)

(At rise: **JACK** *climbs down the beanstalk.* **NARRATORS** *1-3 come out of hiding.)*

NARRATOR 1. And so…

NARRATOR 2. With the giant safely in bed…

NARRATOR 3. The brave and foolish boy climbed down the beanstalk.

*(***NARRATORS** 1-3 *exit.)*

JACK. Mother! I'm home!

*(***MOTHER** *enters.)*

MOTHER. There you are! Where have you been?

JACK. I went to the top of the beanstalk, Mother!

MOTHER. You what?!

JACK. I saw the magical land above the clouds and went on a great, big adventure! A giant tried to eat me!

MOTHER. A giant! That's it! No more adventures for you! Adventures are dangerous, Jack.

JACK. I got us some gold.

MOTHER. All is forgiven. Give me the gold. *(***MOTHER** *grabs the gold.)* Oh Jack, we're rich! It's been so long since there's been gold in this house! Our troubles are over! We can buy food. A lot of food. Heck, we can buy the whole market if we wanted to. And we can fix the house. And pay off all our debts.

JACK. And we can get the cow back!

MOTHER. We'll see.

*(***NARRATOR 4** *enters.)*

NARRATOR 4. But as time went by, so did the money.

MOTHER. Jack, we're broke.

JACK. That's all right Mother. At least we have each other.

MOTHER. Jack, you'll have to climb up that beanstalk and get us more gold.

JACK. We don't need gold, Mother. We have the power to make our dreams come true.

MOTHER. Dreams are expensive, Jack. Now be a good boy and climb up the beanstalk.

JACK. Okay. But first I must change my appearance so the giant's wife won't recognize me.

NARRATOR 4. And so he did.

(**JACK** *becomes* **JACK 2** *- someone completely different.*)

JACK 2. There. That's better.

MOTHER. Be careful, my son. And get me something good!

(**MOTHER** *exits.* **JACK 2** *climbs up the beanstalk.*)

NARRATOR 4. And so Jack climbed up the beanstalk.

(**NARRATOR 4** *exits.*)

(end of scene)

Scene 6

(Setting: The Magical Land Above the Clouds)

(At rise: **JACK 2** *climbs up the beanstalk and arrives at the top.)*

*(***JACK 2** *reaches the top.* **THE ONE THAT GOT AWAY** *runs in, screaming.)*

THE ONE THAT GOT AWAY. What are you crazy? There's a giant! Run for your life!

*(***THE ONE THAT GOT AWAY** *runs off.* **GIANT'S WIFE** *enters.)*

GIANT'S WIFE. A child! Can it be? My dreams have come true!

JACK 2. I already have a mother. I just need a place to hide.

GIANT'S WIFE. Well, you can't hide here. A couple of days ago I let a child into the castle and he stole my husband's stolen gold.

JACK 2. I had a very good reason for stealing that gold. And besides I'm a completely different child.

GIANT'S WIFE. That's true. Come in then but watch yourself. My husband, the giant, he eats children.

JACK 2. I prefer milk myself.

GIANT'S WIFE. You are so cute.

THE GIANT. *(offstage)* Fe fi fo fum! I smell the blood of an Englishmun!

GIANT'S WIFE. My husband! Quick! Hide!

*(***JACK 2** *hides.* **THE GIANT** *enters.)*

THE GIANT. Wife! I smell a child!

GIANT'S WIFE. A child? Where would I get a child at this time of night?

THE GIANT. I know my nose, Wife! There's a child around here somewhere!

GIANT'S WIFE. Are you sure? Maybe you have a cold.

THE GIANT. Wife! Child! Now!

GIANT'S WIFE. Fine.

(**THE GIANT** *and* **GIANT'S WIFE** *look around for* **JACK 2** *as* **JACK 2** *goes from place to place.*)

GIANT'S WIFE. *(looking around)* He's not here.

THE GIANT. He's not here.

JACK 2. *(still hiding)* He's not here.

THE GIANT. He's not anywhere. Maybe I do have a cold.

GIANT'S WIFE. I'll make you some Buffalo Noodle soup.

THE GIANT. I'm too upset to eat. Wife, bring me my hen that lays the golden eggs!

GIANT'S WIFE. Again with the hen! Ever since your stolen gold was stolen you've done nothing but make your hen lay golden eggs. Wouldn't you rather hold hands and look into each other's eyes?

THE GIANT. Wife! Hen! Now!

(**GIANT'S WIFE** *brings in* **HEN**.)

GIANT'S WIFE. Fine. Here's your stupid hen. I'm going for a walk.

(**GIANT'S WIFE** *exits.*)

THE GIANT. Hen! Egg! Now!

(**HEN** *works very hard and finally lays a gold egg.* **THE GIANT** *takes the golden egg.*)

THE GIANT. Hurray! A golden egg! I love golden eggs! They're so shiny! And eggy! Do it again! Do it again!

(**HEN** *sighs and works very, very hard until it finally lays another golden egg.* **THE GIANT** *takes the golden egg.*)

THE GIANT. Another golden egg! Ooooo…shiny…eggy. I must have more!

(**HEN** *gives a great big sigh and works very, very, very hard until it finally lays another golden egg.*)

THE GIANT. Another golden egg!!! More! More! MORE!

(**HEN** *collapses from exhaustion.*)

HEN. Baaawwwkkk…

THE GIANT. Okay, you rest. I'm going to put these eggs somewhere safe. I'll be back for more eggs soon.

HEN. *(very exhausted)* Baaaaawwwwk…

(THE GIANT exits. JACK 2 comes out of hiding.)

JACK 2. Hello there, Hen. My name is Jack. I was wondering if you'd like to come home with me. If you do I promise you'll lay no more than one golden egg a day.

(HEN jumps up to her feet with a great big smile on her beak.)

HEN. Bawk Bawk!

JACK 2. Gosh, Mother sure will be glad to see you. She loves gold.

(JACK 2 puts his arm around HEN. THE GIANT enters.)

THE GIANT. Stop thief! Unhand that hen!

(JACK 2 lets go of HEN. THE GIANT sniffs at the air.)

THE GIANT. Hey…I know that smell. You're the child that stole my stolen gold!

JACK 2. Please, don't eat me.

THE GIANT. Don't be silly. I have to eat you. I'm the giant.

JACK 2. Oh.

(JACK 2 sneaks away during THE GIANT's speech.)

THE GIANT. Eating people is kind of a family tradition. You see, I come from a long line of giants. My father was a giant and his father was a giant, so naturally when I grew up to be big and strong, I took over the family business. It's a really big responsibility, but then again, I'm really big guy, with a really big appetite. Okay, let's eat! *(THE GIANT looks around.)* Hey…where'd he go?

(THE GIANT exits.)

(end of scene)

Scene 7

(Setting: The Miserable Little Shack.

(At rise: **JACK 2** *and the* **HEN** *climb down the beanstalk.)*

*(***NARRATOR 5** *enters.)*

NARRATOR 5. And so the brave hen and the foolish boy got away from the giant and climbed down the beanstalk.

JACK 2. Mother! I'm home!

*(***MOTHER** *enters.)*

MOTHER. There you are my darling boy. What did you bring me?

JACK 2. I brought you a hen!

MOTHER. A hen? You numbskull…I told you to bring me some gold.

JACK 2. But this hen lays golden eggs.

MOTHER. A hen that lays golden eggs! Oh, Jack do you know what this means?

JACK 2. We can make golden omelets!

MOTHER. No, you silly boy…you've found our long lost family fortune!

JACK 2. Our family had a fortune?

MOTHER. It's been lost for a very long time. But it's true, Jack, once our family was filthy rich. We had a hen that could lay eggs of gold and a harp that could sing it's own songs. It was so wonderful, Jack. It was just like a fairytale…but then it all went terribly wrong.

JACK 2. What happened?

MOTHER. A giant came down from the sky and robbed us.

JACK 2. A giant?!

MOTHER. It was horrible, Jack. That nasty, no good giant took everything I loved away from me.

JACK 2. You still had me.

MOTHER. It was horrible…your father swore vengeance and went after the giant himself.

JACK 2. Yeah, and that's when he climbed up the beanstalk and found the giant hiding in his castle and then he kicked the giant's butt and he took back our treasure and we all lived happily ever after…The End.

MOTHER. I wish that were true Jack, but your father never came home to us… *(sobbing)* and neither did the treasure!

JACK 2. Don't be sad, Mother. Today is our magical fairy tale day! We've got the hen back and soon we'll have enough golden eggs to get the cow back!

MOTHER. We don't need the cow, Jack. We need the Magical Singing Harp. It sings it's own songs! Our life would be filled with the most beautiful music.

JACK 2. I could get the harp for you, Mother. I bet it's in the giant's castle. Just like the hen and the gold.

MOTHER. Oh Jack, I couldn't ask you to do something so dangerous.

JACK 2. But you didn't ask, Mother…it was all my idea.

MOTHER. That's true. Good luck.

(**MOTHER** *exits.* **NARRATOR 3** *enters.*)

NARRATOR 3. And so, once again, Jack started the long but familiar journey up the beanstalk…

JACK 2. *(to* **NARRATOR 3***)* Excuse me, but I can't go up the beanstalk just yet. I have to change my appearance so I won't be recognized.

NARRATOR 3. *(sigh)* Fine.

(**JACK 2** *turns into* **JACK 3** – *someone completely different.*)

JACK 3. There. That's better.

NARRATOR 3. And so, once again, Jack started the long but familiar journey up the beanstalk

(**NARRATOR 3** *exits.*)

(end of scene)

Scene 8

(Setting: The Magical Land Above the Clouds)

(At rise: **JACK 3** *reaches the top of the beanstalk.* **THE ONE THAT GOT AWAY** *runs in screaming.)*

THE ONE THAT GOT AWAY. You! Crazy! Giant! Run!

*(***THE ONE THAT GOT AWAY** *runs off.* **GIANT'S WIFE** *enters.)*

JACK 3. Hello there.

GIANT'S WIFE. No! Absolutely not! That dream is done! I am not helping any more children!

JACK 3. Please…I'm very hungry.

GIANT'S WIFE. Oh, why do you all have to be so cute? Do you like milk?

JACK 3. One bowl please.

*(***THE GIANT** *enters.)*

THE GIANT. Fe fi fo fum! I smell the blood of an Englishmun!

*(***JACK 3** *hides.)*

GIANT'S WIFE. My husband's home! Quick! You better – *(pause)* Hey, where did he go?

THE GIANT. Wife! I smell a child!

GIANT'S WIFE. Really? A child? How strange?

THE GIANT. It's probably the same child who stole my gold and my hen!

GIANT'S WIFE. Don't be silly. This child has a very different appearance. Now stop your worrying and go to bed.

THE GIANT. I'm not sleepy!

GIANT'S WIFE. That doesn't matter. It's time to go to bed.

THE GIANT. I am THE GIANT! I do what I want! I WANT MY HARP!

GIANT'S WIFE. Somebody's tired.

THE GIANT. Wife! Harp! Now!

GIANT'S WIFE. Fine. I'll get your stupid harp. *(calling out)* Harp!

*(**HARP** peeks in.)*

HARP. I will not enter until I am properly announced.

*(**HARP** disappears again.)*

GIANT'S WIFE. *(sigh)* Ladies and gentlemen, I am proud to present, the one, the only, the Magical Singing Harp!

*(**THE GIANT** applauds. **JACK 3** appears and applauds too. **HARP** enters and waves to the crowd. **JACK 3** hides again.)*

HARP. Thank you. Thank you all so very much. You're too kind.

GIANT'S WIFE. Ugh! I'm going to my mother's.

*(**GIANT'S WIFE** exits. **HARP** does a vocal warm-up.)*

HARP. Mae, Me, Mi, Mo, Mu…

THE GIANT. Harp! Sing! Now!

HARP. I'd like to begin this evening's performance with a bedtime classic I'm sure you will enjoy.

*(All of the **HARP**'s songs are sung without music.)*

*(**THE GIANT** falls asleep during the song.)*

(Song: ROCK-A-BYE-GIANT)

HARP. *(to the tune of "Rock-A-Bye Baby")*
ROCK-A-BYE GIANT ON THE BEANSTALK.
WHEN THE WIND BLOWS THE GIANT WILL ROCK.
WHEN THE STALK BREAKS THE GIANT WILL FALL.
AND DOWN WILL COME GIANT. HE IS SO TALL.

(end of song)

THE GIANT. *(SNORE!)*

HARP. Asleep. Again. Ugh! I should never open with a lullaby.

JACK 3. Excuse me, Mr. Harp.

HARP. No autographs, please.

JACK 3. Oh no…I don't want your autograph. I want to take you home with me.

HARP. Why should I go home with you? You don't even want my autograph.

JACK 3. My mother loves your music. She's your biggest fan.

HARP. Actually, the giant's my biggest fan.

THE GIANT. *(SNORE!)*

JACK 3. My mother would never fall asleep during one of your performances.

HARP. I like her already. Okay, I'll go home with you.

JACK 3. You will?

HARP. I know. I can hardly believe it myself.

JACK 3. *(very loudly)* Hurray!

THE GIANT. *(waking up)* Hey, what's the big idea?! The child!!!

JACK 3. Uh-oh. Time to go. To the beanstalk!

HARP. But I'm in the middle of my concert…

> (**JACK 3** *grabs* **HARP** *and runs away*)

THE GIANT. Stop! Thief! Unhand that harp!

> (**THE GIANT** *chases after* **JACK 3** *and* **HARP.**)

> (*Song: THE GIANT AND THE THIEF*)

HARP. *(singing to the tune of* "The Farmer in the Dell"*)*
THE THIEF IS GETTING AWAY!
THE THIEF IS GETTING AWAY!
HEIGH HO! AWAY WE GO!
THE THIEF IS GETTING AWAY!

JACK 3. What are you doing?

HARP. I'm singing. That's what I do. Look out! *(singing to the tune of* "The Farmer in the Dell"*)*
THE GIANT'S CATCHING UP!
THE GIANT'S CATCHING UP!
LET'S GO! YOU'RE MUCH TOO SLOW!
THE GIANT'S CATCHING UP!

JACK 3. Please. Stop singing.

THE GIANT. I hear you, my harp! I'm coming!

JACK 3. The giant is following your voice. If you don't stop singing we'll never be able to escape.

HARP. I'm sorry. I can't help myself. I'm the Magical Singing Harp.

JACK 3. Then sing quietly, okay? So we can sneak down the beanstalk.

HARP. Okay. I'll try.

(**NARRATORS** 1-5 *enter.*)

NARRATOR 1. *(whispering)* And so Jack and the Magical Singing Harp climbed down to the bottom of the beanstalk.

(**JACK 3** *and* **HARP** *climb down the beanstalk as* **HARP** *sings.*)

HARP. *(singing softly at first to the tune of* "The Farmer in the Dell".*)*
THE HARP IS SINGING LOW.
THE HARP IS SINGING LOW.

(The singing builds until **HARP** *is singing very loudly.)*

OH NO. A CRESCENDO.
THE HARP IS SINGING LOW!!!!

THE GIANT. My harp! I hear you! I'm coming!

HARP. Sorry.

(The actor playing **THE GIANT** *hides from the audience and does his lines as if he's climbing down the beanstalk.)*

(end of scene)

Scene 9

(Setting: The Miserable Little Shack)

(At rise: **JACK 3** *and* **HARP** *wait at the bottom of the beanstalk.)*

JACK 3. Oh no! The giant's coming down the beanstalk!

HARP.
HE'LL BE COMIN' DOWN THE BEANSTALK WHEN HE COMES!
HE'LL BE COMIN' DOWN THE BEANSTALK –

JACK 3. *(to* **HARP***)* Seriously?!?

HARP. *(gasp!)* The giant's almost to the bottom of the beanstalk!

JACK 3. Oh my gosh! What'll I do?!?

NARRATOR 2. Jack needed an idea and fast.

JACK 3. Wait! I've got an idea! I'll cut down the beanstalk!

HARP. Brilliant!

JACK 3. Now all I need is an axe.

*(***THE ONE THAT GOT AWAY*** runs in screaming with an axe and hands it to* **JACK 3** *before running away.)*

HARP. Boy, that was handy.

JACK 3. Today is my magical fairytale day.

HARP. Oh.

NARRATOR 3. And so Jack went about the business of cutting down the beanstalk.

HARP. *(singing to the tune of "Old MacDonald")*
HERE A CHOP! THERE A CHOP! EVERYWHERE A CHOP CHOP!

*(***JACK 3*** cuts through the beanstalk.)*

JACK 3. Timber!

THE GIANT. *(from his place of hiding)* Uh-oh. No more beanstalk. Giant! Fall! Now!

NARRATOR 4. The giant came down with a terrible crash...

ALL. Boom!

NARRATOR 5. And that was the end of the giant.

ALL. Hurray!

 *(**MOTHER** enters with **HEN**.)*

MOTHER. What's with all this noise and celebration?

NARRATORS 1-5. JACK KILLED THE GIANT!

MOTHER. That's nice. *(to **JACK**)* Did you get the harp?

JACK 3. I sure did. He's right behind me.

 *(**HARP** peeks out.)*

HARP. I will not enter until I am properly announced.

MOTHER. Harp! I can't believe it's really you!

 *(**MOTHER** hugs **HARP**.)*

HARP. Unhand me, woman. You're wrinkling my cape. I said let go!

 *(**THE GIANT** enters rubbing his head.)*

THE GIANT. *(moaning and groaning)* My harp...I hear you... I'm coming...

 *(**THE ONE THAT GOT AWAY** runs in.)*

THE ONE THAT GOT AWAY. The giant! He's alive! Run for your life! He'll eat us all!

THE GIANT. No! Wait! Please! I'm not going to eat anybody.

THE ONE THAT GOT AWAY. You're not?

THE GIANT. No, I'm not. I had some time to think while I was falling from the sky. I realized that just because I'm "THE GIANT" it doesn't mean I have to go around eating people and stealing their treasure. I mean that's the kind of thing that happens in a storybook.

 *(**BEANSELLER** enters with fairytale book.)*

BEANSELLER. That's right and there's more to life than words and pictures, giant. Remember, life's an adventure that's meant to be lived.

JACK 3. *(gasp!)* Page ninety-four! Mother, it's the beanseller!

MOTHER. Jack, it's your father.

JACK 3. My father?!?

THE ONE THAT GOT AWAY. I did not see that coming.

MOTHER. Nigel, where have you been?

BEANSELLER. When I left home those many years ago I promised you that I would not come back until our treasure was returned. Now it's back so here I am.

JACK 3. But why didn't you go and get the treasure yourself?

BEANSELLER. It's a long story.

THE GIANT. Tell! Story! Now!

BEANSELLER. Well…I needed some magic beans so I could grow the beanstalk to get up to the giant, but I couldn't buy them because the giant had taken all my money.

THE GIANT. Sorry about that.

BEANSELLER. It's okay. Anyway, I still needed to get the magic beans, so I stole some from a witch.

JACK 3. Father, you should never steal from a witch. They'll put a spell on you.

JACK 3 and **BEANSELLER.** Page one hundred and seventeen.

BEANSELLER. I know, I know…I should have seen it coming.

MOTHER. A witch put a spell on you?!?

BEANSELLER. Y'up. Now my feet can't leave the ground. **(BEANSELLER** *demonstrates)* See…I can't even jump for joy.

JACK 3. And that's why you couldn't climb up the beanstalk and get the treasure!

BEANSELLER. That's right. I had to wait until you were brave and foolish enough to do it yourself.

MOTHER. He certainly is brave and foolish. Just like his father.

JACK 3. And now the treasure's back and we can be a family again!

HEN. Bawk! Bawk!

(**MOTHER, FATHER, JACK 3, HEN** *and* **HARP** *hug.)*

ALL. Awww…

THE GIANT. *(crying)* BOO-HOO-HOO-HOO!

JACK 3. Giant, why are you crying?

THE GIANT. It's just so beautiful. Family. Together. *(crying more)* I miss my wife!

(**GIANT'S WIFE** *enters.*)

GIANT'S WIFE. I miss you too, pookey!

THE GIANT. Wife! Hug! Now!

(They hug.)

ALL. Awww…

MOTHER. Wait a second, I don't get it. Jack cut down the beanstalk. How did the giant's wife get down here?

GIANT'S WIFE. I took the stairs.

EVERYONE EXCEPT GIANT'S WIFE. THERE ARE STAIRS?!

MOTHER. Doesn't anyone else find this all a bit convenient?

JACK 3. Oh, Mother, anything can happen today. Today is our magical fairytale day.

(**COW** *enters.*)

COW. MOO.

JACK 3. And we got the cow back!

ALL. Hurray!

(end of scene)

End of Play